For my family
D. J. P.

Introduction

We Both Read books can be read alone or with another person. If you are reading the book alone, you can read it like any other book. If you are reading with another person, you can take turns reading aloud. If you are taking turns, the reader with more experience should read the parts marked with a yellow dot ⬤. The reader with less experience should read the parts marked with a blue dot ⬤. As you read, you will notice some difficult words introduced in sections with a yellow dot, then repeated in sections with a blue dot. You can recognize these words by their **bold lettering**.

Sharing the reading of a book can be a lot of fun, and reading aloud is a great way to improve fluency and expression. If you are reading with someone else, you might also want to take the time, while reading the book, to interact and talk about what is happening in the story. After reading with someone else, you might even want to experience reading the entire book on your own.

The Mystery of Pirate's Point

A We Both Read Chapter Book: Level 3
Guided Reading Level: P (Reader 1) and N (Reader 2)

———————————————

Text Copyright © 2007 by D. J. Panec
Illustrations Copyright © 2007 by Brie Spangler
All rights reserved

We Both Read® is a trademark of Treasure Bay, Inc.

Published by Treasure Bay, Inc.
P. O. Box 119
Novato, CA 94948 USA

Printed in Malaysia

Library of Congress Catalog Card Number: 2007920852

ISBN: 978-1-60115-010-3

Visit us online at:
www.WeBothRead.com

PR-11-19

The Mystery
of Pirate's Point

By D. J. Panec

Illustrated by Brie Spangler

Contents

TREASURE BAY

Chapter 1
Out of Lucky

It was just after lunch at Camp Miggles when the swim coach burst into our cabin with a big grin on his face. I looked up from my comic book. Neither I nor my best friends, Aaron and Marcus, were good swimmers, so I kind of doubted Coach **Coburn** was there for us.

"I have great news!" he said. "Alex and John have been chosen for the boy's swim team this year. You're the only cabin with two boys to make the Pirates team!" He looked over at John and Alex. "The annual relay race against the girl's team is in three days, so I want both of you down at the lake first thing in the morning for some serious training."

Now, this was something to get excited about! For some reason, the girls here at camp were being very competitive. Every time you turned around they were talking about something they had just won or done better than the boys. In fact, just that morning, I had seen two boys suffer an **embarrassing** loss in a game of Ping-Pong. The girls who had won acted like this was final proof that girls were the dominant life form on the planet. It was getting pretty annoying.

"That's the best news I've heard all summer!" I said. "You guys are incredible swimmers. I'm sure you can win this for the Pirates!"

"Thanks, Sam," said Alex. "I hope you're right."

"I hope you're right too, Sam," said Coach **Coburn**. "The last four years have been pretty **embarrassing**. I'd hate to see the Pirates lose to the Dolphins again this year."

At dinner that night, Alex and John told us the whole terrible story.

"My brother was at camp here five years ago," Alex said. "That's when the Pirates last won the swim relay. The race was really close that year. Just as the swimmers were on their last lap from Pirate's Point to the pier, a bird did a big one right on the judge's head."

"I always wondered how Mr. Collins got the name Poopy Head," said Aaron.

Alex continued, "Well, some of the girls thought that they had won the race, but old Poopy Head gave the win to the Pirates."

John nodded. "The Pirates had a team mascot named Lucky. It was a wooden parrot that the first Pirates team made a long time ago."

"Well, no one thought it was just a **coincidence** when, two days after the race, Lucky suddenly disappeared," said Alex.

He glanced over at the tables full of girls and whispered, "Everyone thought that a certain group of sore losers stole him, but no one could ever prove anything."

"Lucky's never been seen since, and the Pirates have never won the swim relay since then either," John said, shaking his head. "Maybe losing Lucky and losing all those races was a **coincidence**, but I wish we had our old mascot back."

"If we had Lucky back, I'm sure we could win," Alex said.

"There's one other thing," said John. "Whoever took Lucky left a note behind. It said, 'You will treasure the picture to Pirate's Point.' Some guys thought it was a clue, but if it *was* a clue, no one ever figured it out."

The next morning, I found myself pushing gooey **scrambled** eggs around my plate, while Aaron kept talking nonstop about the missing parrot. "Come on, Sam!" he said. "Maybe we *can* find Lucky. You heard Alex. If they had their mascot back, they'd win the race for sure! We can't let those *girls* win!"

"And what's the problem with *girls* winning?" said a voice behind us. We turned. There stood a redheaded girl staring at Aaron like he had just said something terrible about her best friend.

Aaron stammered, "Uh, nothing. I mean, that is, if they win. But . . ."

"Oh, the Dolphins are going to win. *That* you can be sure of." Then she whipped around and headed toward the next table.

"Boy, *some* people are touchy," said Aaron as he made a funny face at the table full of girls.

"Listen, Aaron," I said, "I'd love to find Lucky, but it's been five years! If they couldn't find him back then, what makes you think we can find him now?"

Just then, I felt the cold wet slap of **scrambled** eggs hitting the side of my head. I whipped around to see all the girls at the next table giggling into their plates. Except one. The redheaded girl looked at me and smiled. "Oops," she said. "Sorry. I'm just a girl, so my aim isn't very good." And then the girls started laughing and falling all over each other.

That's when I saw Marcus flick a spoonful of his eggs. Maybe he was just lucky, but the redhead got it right between the eyes.

Chapter 2
The Clue in the Office

"I don't care who started it!" shouted Ms. Hammer. She was the head counselor and terror of the camp. "If any of you throw so much as a pea in this camp again, I'm going to fry you up and serve you for breakfast. Now get back in there and start cleaning it all up. March!"

We slumped back to the dining room liked spanked puppies. "Wow. I can't believe that not one of those girls got pulled in. How come we had to take the rap for that?" groused Aaron.

"You're right," I said. "It's not fair." I looked over at Marcus for agreement, but he seemed lost in his own thoughts.

"Guys, did you see the note pinned to Hammer's bulletin board?" he asked.

"No," I said. "What note?"

The note. The one from five years ago. It's pinned to Hammer's board. But there was something strange about it."

"Hey!" shouted the cook from the kitchen. "The only thing I want to hear out there is the sound of you guys cleaning."

Later that day, we went down to the lake to watch the Pirates training. Alex and John were just getting out of the water. I was sure they had been swimming a long time because they looked dead tired.

Suddenly, I heard a big cheer. I turned, thinking that maybe they were cheering for our guys. It was girls cheering—the ones who had started the food fight. The redhead was holding what looked like a **weird** stuffed shark with its tail fin on wrong. She held it up in the air and all the girls started chanting, "Dolphins win 'cuz Pirates can't swim!"

I looked at the lake and in fairness I have to say that the girls' team was doing a pretty good job of cutting through the water. Alex was looking a bit glum. And it definitely didn't help when Aaron slapped him on the back and said, "Come on. You aren't going to let a bunch of girls beat you!"

"Aaron!" Marcus hissed. "I can't believe you said that!"

Aaron shrugged. "Said what?"

I just rolled my eyes and shook my head.

Late that same night, I was having a very strange dream. The redhead was throwing ice cream at me and she was chanting, "Sam only drools, while redheads rule!" It was pretty **weird**. Then she was shaking me and I really started to get scared.

But it was Marcus shaking me. "Sam, wake up! I think I have an idea on the note."

"Note? What note?" I said, checking myself, half expecting to be covered in ice cream.

"*The* note!!" he hissed.

○ "Look," he said. He held out a piece of paper as Aaron stumbled over to join us. Written on the paper was, "You will treasure the picture to pirate's point."

"See? That's just how the real note was written, the one I saw in Hammer's office, but the **sentence** doesn't really make sense. If it was talking about Pirate's Point, it should be capitalized and it would say '*of* Pirate's Point' instead of '*to* pirate's point.'"

"So?" said Aaron. "The girls who wrote it didn't have good grammar. How does that help us?"

"Maybe they had perfect grammar," Marcus said, grinning, "but the words need to be rearranged."

Now I got excited! "OK, let's see what else we can make of this **sentence**," I said. "Let's write each word on a separate piece of paper."

We moved the words around and came up with a couple of different **sentences**. And one of them sounded like it might be the real clue!

(I'll tell you what we came up with, but, if you'd like, you can try it yourself first. Just try putting the words in a different order and see if something sounds like it might be a clue.)

Chapter 3
The Real Clue

I noticed that the words could be rearranged to read, "Treasure will point you to the pirate's picture," but that didn't make much sense as a clue. Then Marcus pointed out that it could read, "The pirate's picture will point you to treasure."

"I'll bet you that's it!" Aaron said. We all agreed that this could be the real clue.

"Unfortunately," he said, slumping down on my bunk, "we have no idea what 'the pirate's picture' could be."

We still didn't have any more ideas by lunch the next day. As we were leaving the dining hall, we evaded the **counselors** grabbing victims for arts and crafts but then found ourselves facing the Dolphins cheering section sitting behind a table.

"Would you like to sign our **petition**?" asked that same redhead.

"It's a **petition** to change the name of Pirate's Point to Dolphin's Snout," she added.

"What?" I said, staring at her.

She smiled and said, "Well, don't you think it's fair? The Dolphins have won the race five years in a row now."

Suddenly, my brain stopped working. I wanted so badly to stun her with a witty comeback line, but I couldn't think of a thing to say. I was just standing there with my mouth open. Fortunately, one of the **counselors** appeared. "Just the guys I've been looking for," he said. "Come on. I need more volunteers to work on skits for the campfire."

"OK, now you can use anything you see here to help with your skit," said the counselor, gesturing toward boxes full of props and costumes.

"This stuff looks like it's been beaten up in skits for the last twenty years," said Marcus, holding up an old pirate hat.

"Hey, let's do a pirate skit," **exclaimed** Aaron as he pulled out a toy sword.

We rummaged through the boxes and found a lot of cool pirate stuff. I was really getting into this.

● "Aaar! Come on, me mateys!" I shouted in my best pirate's voice. And then all three of us shouted, "Aaar!" together and struck a really good pirate's pose.

The counselor came over and **exclaimed**, "That's fabulous! That'll make a great photo for the camp newsletter."

Then suddenly, I had an idea. "Hey!" I shouted. "I know where we might find a pirate's picture!"

○ "I'm afraid you will have to ask Ms. Hammer," said her stuffy assistant just as the terror of the camp walked through the door.

"Ask me what?" she demanded, staring hard at Marcus, Aaron, and me.

"Well," I said, "we were wondering if we could see the old **issues** of the camp newsletter."

"Why?" she asked, squinting her eyes.

"Uh, we're doing research on the history of the camp," Marcus said bravely. "For a skit we're doing."

"Well, it better be a good skit," she said, gesturing into the corner. "Look in those **cabinets**."

Pirates Win the Big Race!

Lucky the Mascot Reported Missing

Campfire Skits are a Big Hit.

As she closed her door, we turned to the old **cabinets** in the corner.

It didn't take long to find the **issues** from five years ago. We hit gold when Aaron picked up an **issue** with the headline "Pirates Win the Big Race!" Right next to this was a story about the campfire skits—and a photo of three girls dressed up like pirates.

"A pirate's picture!" I said. "This has to be it!"

Marcus repeated the words of the clue, "The pirate's picture will point you to treasure."

"Look where she's pointing!" shouted Aaron. "They hid Lucky inside the buffalo head!"

Chapter 4
A Pirate's Puzzle

Just after lights-out that night, Aaron, Marcus, and I snuck out of our cabin and crept down to the dining hall. We were sure that, even after five long years, the parrot was still there inside the buffalo head.

"This is really heavy!" whispered Marcus as he and I lowered the shaggy old head onto a table.

We **carefully** turned it over, and I pointed my flashlight into the big hole in the back. "Nothing!" exclaimed Marcus with disbelief.

None of us could believe it. I took out the newsletter and we looked again at the picture. "Maybe this isn't the right picture," said Marcus.

I looked **carefully** at the photo. "Or maybe . . . it's right where she's pointing," I said. "She's pointing right at the nose."

"Come on, Sam," protested Aaron. "The parrot isn't in the buffalo's nose."

"But maybe something else is!" said Marcus with a sly grin.

"Well, I'm not sticking my finger up his nose to find out!" said Aaron.

"OK. I'll do it," I said. I closed my eyes as I shoved two fingers up one of his nasty nostrils. "Nothing," I said as I pulled my fingers out and began digging them into his other nostril. I flinched as I felt something cold and damp.

Slowly, I pulled out a rolled-up piece of paper! I carefully unrolled it and read the note:

We're better swimmers than you are
And we're even better pirates!
If you want to find your lucky parrot,
you're going to have to look for it.

Yo, ho, ho!
60 feet East.
60 feet West.
We're gonna see,
who's really the best!

"60 feet east and 60 feet west! This is definitely another clue," said Marcus.

Suddenly, the lights turned on in the dining hall. We all turned and froze. "What are you boys doing with our buffalo head?" boomed the angry voice of Ms. Hammer.

Busted! Busted, big time.

Chapter 5
Mud Pies for Lunch

"Sorry you can't be there," said Alex the next day as he and John prepared to leave for the relay race. Marcus, Aaron, and I had been sentenced to a time-out in our cabin for the entire day.

"Good luck!" I said. They were looking a bit glum, so I added, "I still think you guys can win, but even if you don't, we'll know you did your best."

As we watched Alex and John walk off in the **direction** of the lake, Aaron started in again, "This is so unfair! Plus, I think it's against the law for us to be kept here against our will."

"Yeah, you tell Ms. Hammer exactly that," said Marcus, who looked as defeated as I'd ever seen him.

⬤ "Plus, that clue doesn't make any sense at all," said Aaron. "If you go 60 feet in one **direction** and then 60 feet back, you end up in the same place. What's the point of that?"

As I looked out at the dining hall, it suddenly hit me. "Maybe you don't end up in the same place," I said slowly, thinking hard. "Look at the dining hall."

(Now, if you look carefully at the picture of the dining hall, maybe you can guess what I was thinking before you turn the page!)

"Look," I said. "The dining hall is raised off the ground. And there's a crawl space underneath. If you went 60 feet east from the buffalo head, you'd be standing on the ground out front. Then 60 feet west and you'd be back at the buffalo head again—unless you stayed on the ground! Then, you'd be underneath the floor, right below the buffalo head!"

"They buried the parrot!" shouted Marcus, holding up the old newsletter. "It's right under where they're standing in the picture!"

"Look!" Aaron shouted. "This girl is even holding a shovel!"

"And I'll bet Lucky's in this treasure chest," Marcus added, pointing at the picture.

Just then, the redheaded girl and her friend walked by. "Hi, guys!" she said, tossing her hair back. "I heard you were very bad boys last night. I can't believe Ms. Hammer caught you trying to steal the buffalo head," she said, laughing. "Well, sorry you won't be there to see the Dolphins win the race." And off they went.

"That's it. Come on, guys!" said Aaron heading for the door. "The Pirates can't win the race without Lucky! We've got to dig up that chest!"

"Whoa. Slow down," I said. "We're grounded here. If we walk out, we'll definitely get caught and then we'll be in even more trouble. What we need is a plan."

"A plan?" shouted Aaron. "We don't have time for a plan!"

"Look, the race doesn't start until ten," I said. "We still have some time. We need an excuse to get out of here and get closer to the dining hall. Now, let's think."

Then I saw Marcus grinning. "Isn't the nurse's office next to the dining hall?" he asked.

"Yeah, it's in the back. In fact, it's in the same building," I said, holding my stomach. "And frankly, I'm not feeling very good. I think I need to see the nurse."

"OK, guys," said Aaron, joining in. "If we do this, we're going to have to make it look real." He held up a bottle of water. "We're going to need some dirt."

Ten minutes later the nurse came running into our cabin. "What's this I hear about you all eating mud?" she said. She didn't sound very sympathetic, standing there with her hands on her hips.

"We made a little bet about who could eat the most mud," I said weakly, clutching my stomach.

"I don't feel very well," said Marcus, who really looked like he was about to lose it.

"Okay," sighed the nurse. "If you can walk, come with me."

As we walked out, she shook her head and said, "I would have thought you'd have given up eating mud back when you were in diapers."

In her office, she made us each take two tablespoons of some very foul-tasting liquid. Then she told us to lie down on some cots.

"If you need to use the restroom—and I'm pretty sure you will need to very soon—you can use the restroom just outside," she said. "Now, I'm the safety person for the race, so I've got to go down to the lake. If you need me, just call me on this walkie-talkie. If I don't answer, you'll have to come down to the lake to find me. Otherwise, I want you to stay right here until I get back." She handed me the walkie-talkie and she was gone.

"Now, I really am sick," moaned Marcus.

"Oh, boy. I gotta go," said Aaron, bolting for the door.

Chapter 6
Race to the Finish

At first, all we could think about was making it to the bathroom in time. However, after two or three trips each, we started to feel a lot better.

"Okay," I said, "it's time to do some digging. I think they have some shovels in the shed over there."

"You know," Aaron said, "we really are going to get in a lot of trouble if we get caught."

"No, we won't," said Marcus. "The nurse said to stay here. She didn't tell us to stay here *above* the floor. We're just going to be here *under* the floor."

"Yes, I'm sure Hammer would agree with your logic, Marcus," I said. "Now, are we going?"

Just then, the walkie-talkie came on. "How are you boys doing?"

I pushed the button. "Doing better."

"Well, it's going to be a bit noisy down here, so I'm not sure I'll hear if you call." In the background, I could hear the sound of the race about to start.

"Don't worry," I said. "If you don't answer, I'm sure we can make it down there if we have to. Over."

"OK," she said. "You boys get some rest."

I turned to the guys. "Let's go!"

Everyone was down at the lake, so we had no problem getting shovels and sneaking into the crawl space under the dining room without being spotted.

"The buffalo head is above the fireplace, so we need to get back there where those bricks are," Marcus said, pointing.

"This is nasty," said Aaron as he swept away the spider-webs.

Soon we were all digging as fast as we could. And in just a few minutes we heard a big "Thunk!" as my shovel hit something that sounded like wood.

We pulled out the chest and opened it. There inside was Lucky, just where those pirate girls placed him five long years ago!

"Wahoo!" screamed Marcus as he punched both Aaron and me in the **shoulder**. "We did it!"

"Let's get Lucky down to the lake!" I yelled, and we ran as fast as we could.

As we ran onto the **pier**, I heard the announcer saying, "The Dolphins are in the lead as they approach the finish!"

I held Lucky up high and yelled, "Go, Pirates!" All the guys at the **pier** cheered and we all started chanting, "Go, Pirates! Go, Pirates!"

Aaron and Marcus lifted me up on their **shoulders**, and I could see Alex swimming in toward the **pier.** I yelled, "Come on, Alex. We got Lucky back!" He looked up from the water for a moment. Then suddenly, he turned on the speed and started swimming faster than anyone I have ever seen.

As Alex touched the pier ahead of the lead girl, I thought I might go deaf with the sound of all the guys cheering. A couple of guys lifted Alex onto their shoulders. What a victory!

That's when Ms. Hammer stepped forward. "Aren't you boys supposed to be in your cabin?"

Aaron answered as he held up the walkie-talkie. "The nurse told us to come down to the lake if she didn't answer."

Ms. Hammer turned to the nurse, who shouted, "I'm certainly glad to see you boys are feeling much better."

Alex yelled, "The party's in our cabin!" Another cheer rose from the guys, and we all charged up the hill with me carrying Lucky up high.

That was maybe the best day of my whole life. Every guy in the camp was so happy. Marcus, Aaron, and I got to sit with the Pirates team at the head table. As I looked around, I knew it didn't get any better than this.

That's when I got hit in the neck with a pea. I turned just in time to see that redheaded girl spin in her seat as her girl-friend started in on another giggling fit.

Marcus leaned in and whispered, "By the way, her name is Megan."

"Hey," I said, "I don't care *what* her name is."

"Oh, yeah?" Aaron laughed. "Then how come you know who he's talking about? And how come you're turning all pink?"

Marcus seemed to think this was just as funny as Aaron did. I definitely needed to change the subject before this got out of hand.

"It sure is great to have Lucky back, isn't it?" I said, picking up our treasured parrot.

"Hey!" said Aaron. "I've got a great idea. Why don't we snatch that Dolphin mascot they've got and bury it, just like they did to Lucky."

"OK, wait a minute," jumped in Marcus. "First off, *they* didn't do anything to Lucky. It was some other girls, five years ago. And second, I don't think we should make this an "eye for an eye" kind of thing. That's how some wars get started. One side does something nasty, and then the other side does something nastier, and pretty soon—boom!"

"I have to side with Marcus on this one," I said.

"Yeah, OK," said Aaron. "But it would have been fun. We even could have left clues and everything."

"Clues for what?" said someone behind us.

We all turned. It was that redhead!

Aaron looked like a deer caught in the headlights. "Uh, uh . . . Clue," he stammered. "We were thinking of playing Clue . . . later tonight."

She didn't look like she was buying that, but she just turned to Marcus and me. For a moment she looked like she didn't know what to say, but she finally spurted out, "Anyway, I just wanted to congratulate you on finding Lucky . . . and your team for winning the race."

Now, that wasn't what I expected. Not at all. She stood there for a moment and then turned to leave. Finally, I managed to say, "Uh, thanks. Thanks. That's very nice of you . . . Megan." She seemed surprised that I knew her name.

Then Marcus said with a big grin, "Hey, Megan, would you and your friend like to join us for a game of Clue tonight?"

For a moment, she seemed surprised and embarrassed. But that was over quickly. She smiled and said, "I have to check with my friend, but I think we'll be up for **humiliating** you boys this evening." And with a toss of her hair, she was gone.

After an awkward moment of silence, Aaron said, "So do you think they practice tossing their hair like that, or do you think it just comes naturally to their species?"

"She wasn't tossing her hair!" I said hotly. I couldn't believe I had said that. Aaron and Marcus slowly turned to me, then glanced at each other and burst out laughing.

I am happy to report that we were not **humiliated** that evening. Marcus and I each won a game. To be fair, I have to say that Megan did win the first game, and her friend, Alicia, won the second. But they just couldn't take the pressure and we won the last two games!

As we headed back to our cabin that night, I realized it was only three weeks before Marcus, Aaron, and I would be back at school. I couldn't wait to tell everyone back home about the mystery and how we found Lucky buried under the dining hall. And I couldn't help wondering if we would ever find ourselves involved in another mystery.

If you liked *The Mystery of Pirate's Point*,
here is another We Both Read® book you are sure to enjoy!

Ben and Becky set out to solve the mystery of a
haunted house and find their lost grandfather. All
of them are spending the night in an old mansion,
but in the middle of the night their grandfather suddenly disappears. Now, Ben and Becky are hearing
a strange howling coming from the attic. Are the
stories about the old ghost really true?